Turtle Summer

A Journal for my Daughter

Mary Alice Monroe
Barbara J. Bergwerf

Thanks to:

Barbara Schroeder of NOAA's
National Marine Fisheries Service–
Office of Protected Resources
for verifying the accuracy
of the information in this book

Educators and husbandry staff at the
South Carolina Aquarium
for identifying shells, birds, and plants

Nicholas Johannes for his "day nester" photos
Kelly Thorvalson, and

Susan and Lauren Geddings for their help modeling

Publisher's Cataloging-In-Publication Data
Monroe, Mary Alice.
Turtle summer : a journal for my daughter / Mary Alice Monroe ;
[photographs by] Barbara J. Bergwerf ; sketches, illustrations,
and layout design by Lisa Downey.
[32] p. : col. ill. ; cm.
ISBN: 978-0-97774-2356 (hardcover)
ISBN: 978-1-60718-5833 (pbk.)
1. Loggerhead turtle--Atlantic Coast (U.S.)--Juvenile literature. 2. Sea turtles--Atlantic
Coast (U.S.)--Juvenile literature. 3. Loggerhead turtle.
4. Sea turtles. I. Bergwerf, Barbara J. II. Downey, Lisa. III. Title.
QL666.C536 M66 2007
597.92/80975   2006938664

Also available in Spanish: *La tortuga de verano: Un diario para mi hija*
Spanish paperback ISBN: 978-1-62855-3680

Manufactured in China, December 2016
This product conforms to CPSIA 2008
Seventh Printing

Arbordale Publishing
formerly Sylvan Dell Publishing
Mt. Pleasant, SC 29464
www.ArbordalePublishing.com

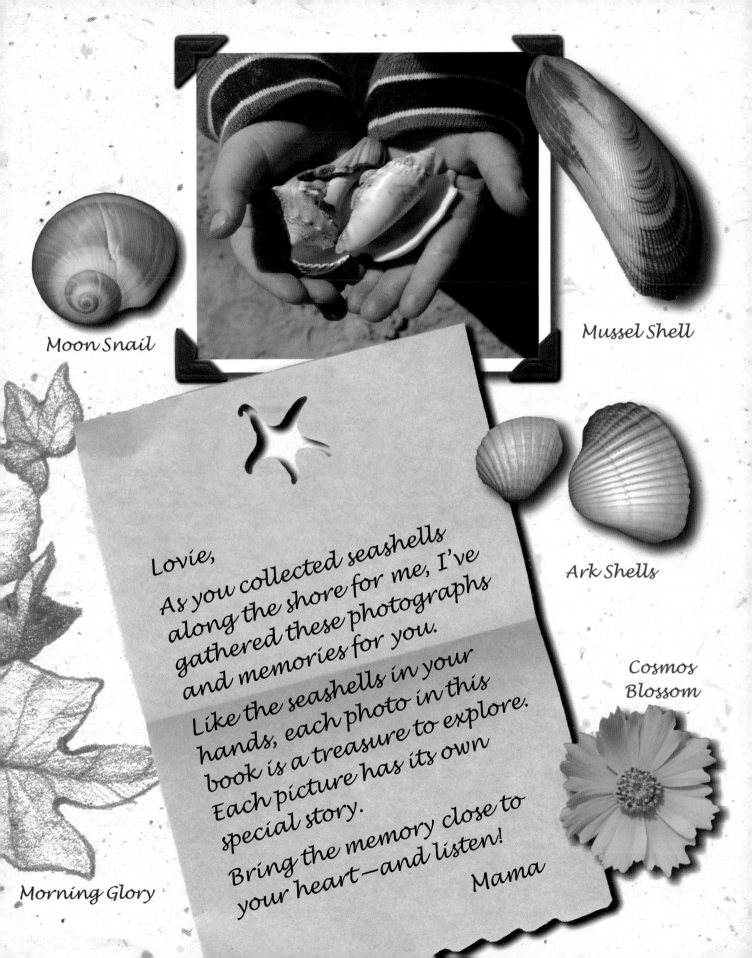

Moon Snail

Mussel Shell

Ark Shells

Cosmos Blossom

Morning Glory

Lovie,

As you collected seashells along the shore for me, I've gathered these photographs and memories for you.

Like the seashells in your hands, each photo in this book is a treasure to explore. Each picture has its own special story.

Bring the memory close to your heart—and listen!

Mama

Primroses

Path to the beach

Clam Shell

Firewheel or
Indian Blanket

Black Skimmers

It is May and the loggerhead sea turtles are returning to our island to lay their eggs.

Every day we walk together from the beach house to sit on our favorite dune.

We watch, and wait, and wonder . . .

Are the turtles out there in the rolling swells?
When will they come ashore?

You are my helper on the Island Turtle Team.
You are eager to learn about the sea turtles,
the flowers, the shells, the birds,
and all things great and small.

I hope that I can teach you—
as a dear lady once taught me—
to not merely know nature but
also to feel nature.

Primrose Cottage

Beach Evening
Primrose

Lettered
Olive Shell

Tulip Shell

May

Sunday	Monday	Tuesday	Wednesday	Thursday	Friday
1	2	3	4	5	6
8	9	10	11	12	13
15	16	17	18		
22					

Only the female turtles leave their home, the great sea, to lay their eggs on the beach of their birth.

With a tank-like crawl, the turtle drags herself to a site high on the beach.

One night we watched a loggerhead come ashore. We hunkered low and kept our distance so not to disturb her. If startled by humans, other animals, or lights, the loggerhead won't lay her eggs.

The mother turtle spends hours digging deep into the sand then laying her eggs. When finished, she leaves for the sea, never to return to her nest.

Dropping her eggs

Each morning, when the sun is still pink on the horizon, volunteers walk the beach on the lookout for turtle tracks!

The turtle team studies the field signs and finds the eggs.

You said the turtle tracks look like tire tracks!

Pennywort

Jack Knife Clam

Slipper Shell

If the nest is in a safe place, we mark it with an orange sign saying that the nest is protected by federal law.

If the nest lies below the high tide line, I dig down to the eggs in the soft, moist sand. I carefully lift the eggs from the nest and place them into our red bucket. Then I carry the precious eggs to a spot higher on the beach.

I use a shell to dig a nest that will be the same size and shape as the loggerhead's nest.

A digging shell

20 inches deep

You think the eggs look like
ping-pong balls!

Our red bucket

A large Cockle Shell

Beach Treasures

The southern sand
dollar has five
slashes in the shell.

Beach
Evening Primrose

Now we wait . . .

After the nests are laid, we wait 55 to 65 days for the eggs to incubate. While waiting, we search for seashells and other beach treasures.

Sand dollars and sea stars are washed ashore by strong surf. If the sand dollar is green with bristly hair, it's alive!

If a sea star loses a leg, it will grow it back.

You carefully put the living sand dollars and sea stars back into the water.

Sea Star

Silver Croton

If you pick up a sea star and see hundreds of tiny feet waving—it is alive!

While we wait, we watch the shorebirds.

Royal Tern

American Oystercatcher

Black Skimmers

Sanderlings

Ring-Billed Gull

Pelican

While we wait, we visit the Sea Turtle Hospital. I work at the aquarium and help sick sea turtles get well.

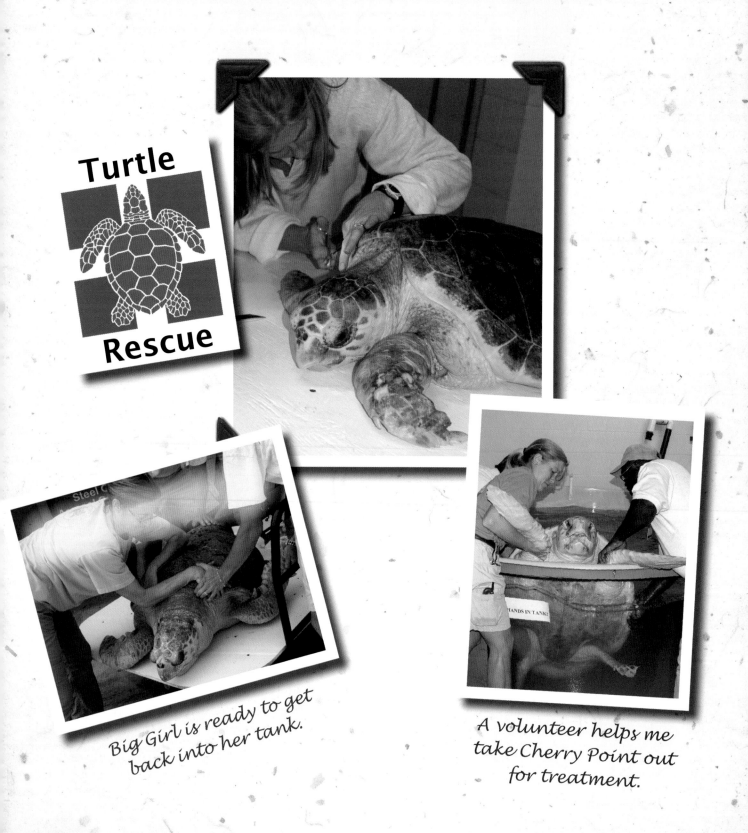

Turtle Rescue

Big Girl is ready to get back into her tank.

A volunteer helps me take Cherry Point out for treatment.

Volunteers help me to clean the wounds and shells, give the turtles their medicine, and scrub the tanks. We all feed and love the turtles.

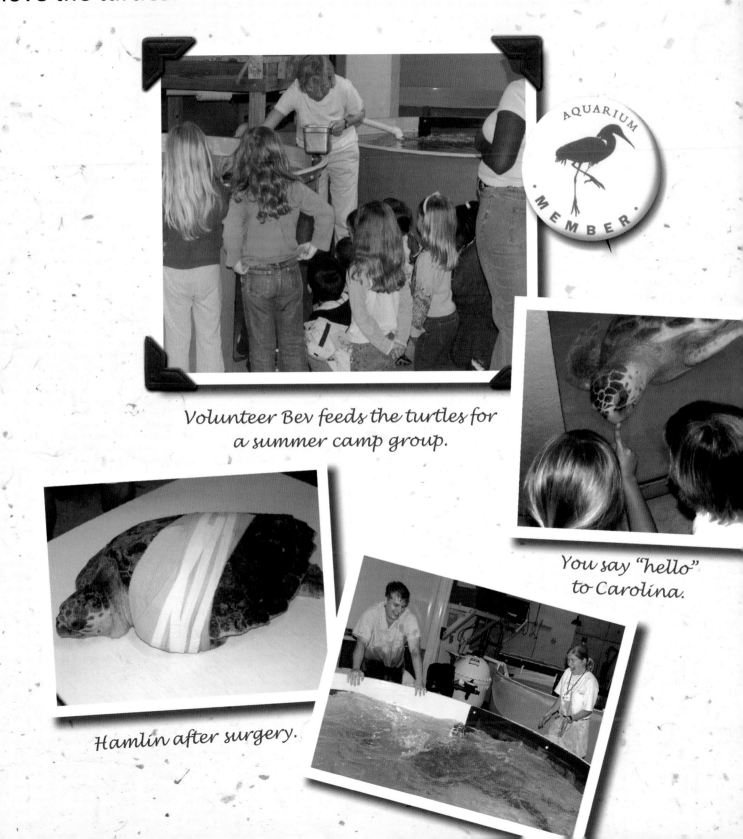

Volunteer Bev feeds the turtles for a summer camp group.

You say "hello" to Carolina.

Hamlin after surgery.

The first nests begin to hatch in July. It's a busy time for us. In the mornings, we look for turtle tracks. In the evenings, we sit by the nests hoping for hatchlings.

Nights by the ocean are breathtakingly black and beautiful.

Sometimes we wonder what the turtles
are doing under the sand . . .

Are they awake?
Are they sleeping?
Are they dreaming?

Deep in the sand, the baby turtles break through their eggshells and work together to dig upward in the sand. They rise to the surface like an elevator.

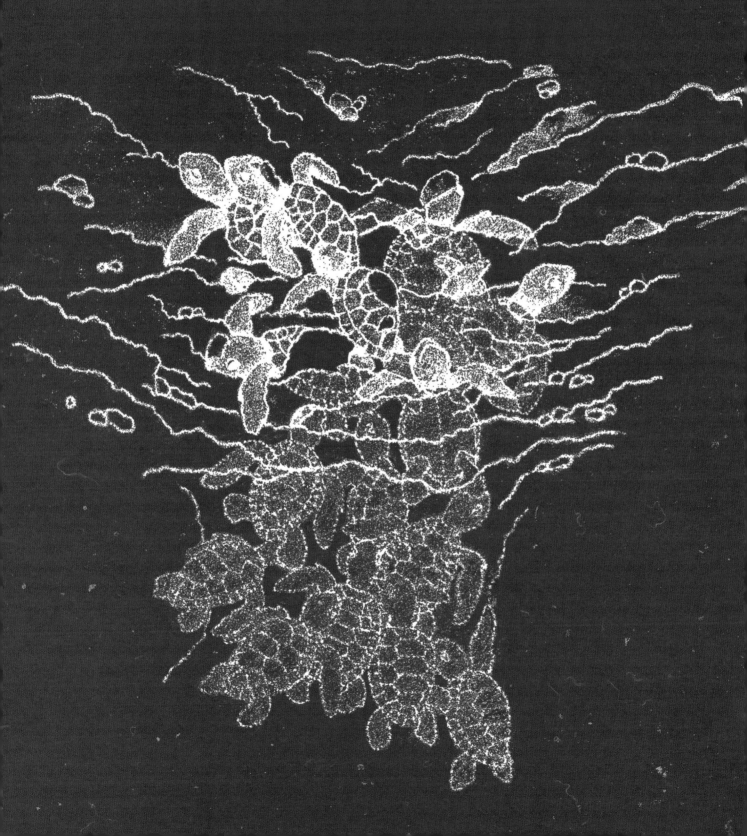

Our first sign that a nest is hatching is a concave circle in the sand. You always ask me when the nest will hatch. I always answer that I don't know.

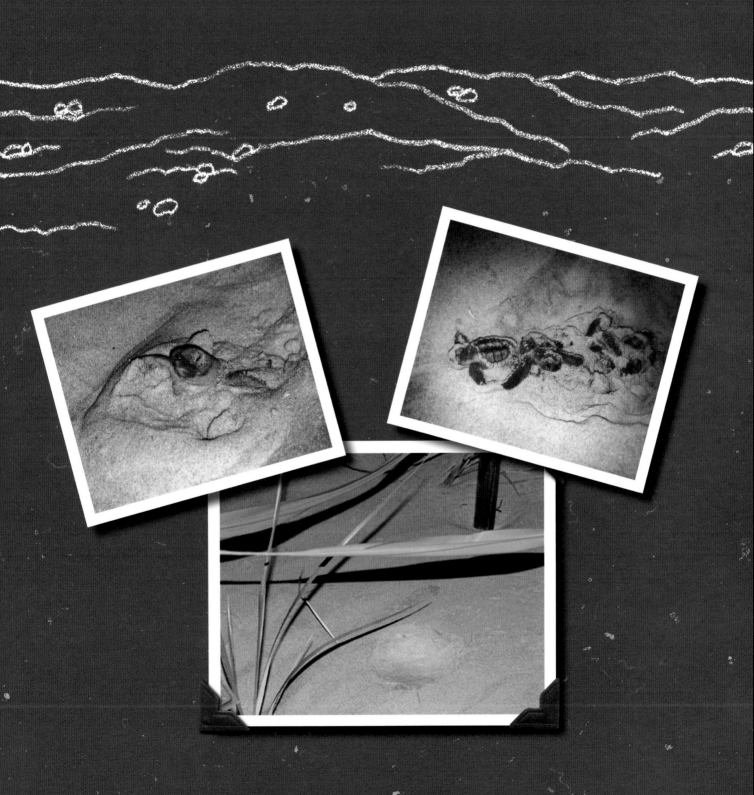

The hatchlings usually emerge from the nest at night when the sand is cool. Sometimes, they come out slowly over a couple of nights. When they charge out in a wiggling mass, we call it a "boil" because it resembles a pot boiling over.

Instinct guides the hatchlings toward the brightest light. In nature, it is the open horizon with the reflection of moonlight or starlight on the ocean. The bright lights from houses, streetlights, and white flashlights confuse them and lead them away from the sea to a certain death.

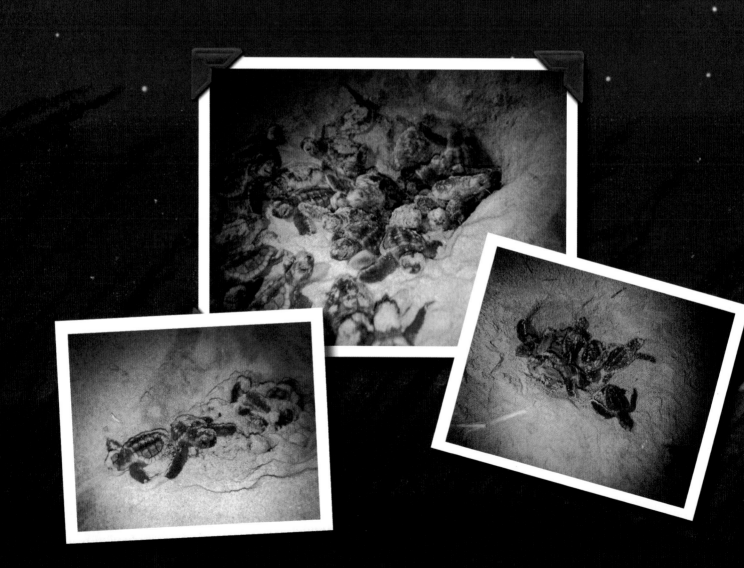

August: Nest Inventory

Three days after hatchlings emerge from their nests, the Turtle Team does an early morning nest inventory. We record the number of hatched and unhatched eggs.

You get excited when we find some sleepy hatchlings in a nest.

In the sunlight, we can watch the hatchlings scramble to the sea. They raise their heads, as if sniffing the direction home or hearing the ancient turtle mother's call.

The hatchlings must crawl across the beach to the sea for imprinting. They stop to rest along the way. You know not to touch or carry them.

Once the hatchlings reach the water, their dive instincts kick in. The turtles swim off, disappearing in the waves.

Goodbye and good luck!

The hatchlings leave our beach to begin a long journey. Not all will survive the many dangers in the great sea. After 30 years, the adult female turtle will return to our beach to nest. She will have grown from three inches to over three feet and weigh up to 350 pounds!

You will have grown up by then, too. I smile and think how you will return home to visit me, just like the loggerhead.

Once again, you and I will be together to watch . . . and wait . . . and to welcome the sea turtle home.

Loggerhead Nesting Fun Facts:

Field signs of a nest:

    ingoing and outgoing tracks
    body pit
    thrown sand
    broken vegetation
    a departing scarp in sand where she turned

On average, the loggerhead lays four nests a summer about two weeks apart.

She lays between 80 and 150 eggs in each nest. *If she lays 100 eggs in each nest and lays four nests in the summer, how many eggs will she lay?*

The sea turtle lays so many eggs to make sure that some of the hatchlings will survive.

The eggs look like ping-pong balls! They are leathery so they won't break when they are laid in the nest.

She doesn't lay eggs every year. She lays nests every two or three years.

After laying all of her eggs, she returns to the sea and will never see or know the hatchlings.

Female sea turtles return to the same area where they hatched to lay their eggs.

Scientist don't know how the turtles find their way "home" to lay their eggs but think that the hatchlings "imprint" the area when they walk from the nest to the ocean. For that reason, it is important to let the hatchlings walk across the beach and not carry them.

If people make loud noises, shine flashlights on the beach, or try to get close to and touch the sea turtle as she comes ashore, she may turn around and leave without nesting. If you are lucky enough to see a sea turtle coming out of the ocean, be quiet and stay at a distance. Don't turn on your flashlight! Let your eyes adapt to the night light.

Sometimes ghost crabs or ants will harm the eggs in the nest.

The mother turtle or the hatchings might have a difficult time going around sand castles or big holes dug in the sand. If you play in the sand at the beach, smooth it all out before you leave. *Remember; only leave your footprints on the beach!*

Sea turtles find their way to the ocean by moving toward the brightest, most open horizon, which under natural conditions is toward the ocean. Bright lights may cause the turtles to crawl the wrong way to certain death. If you are at the beach, turn off the outside lights and pull curtains down at night to keep the beach dark.

Sea turtles like to eat jellyfish and sometimes mistake floating plastic for a jellyfish. Would you get sick if you ate a plastic bag or a deflated balloon? Pick up all plastic and trash – even if you are not close to the ocean.

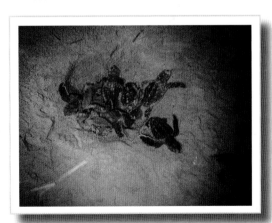

Items Needed During Turtle Nesting Matching Activity

Match the items needed during turtle nesting season. Answers are upside down on the bottom of the page.

1. These mark the nest to let people know not to disturb it or walk on it.

2. If we have to move the nest to a better spot, we use this to hold the eggs as we move them.

3. This protects the nest from raccoons or other animals that might try to dig up the eggs. The holes are big enough for the hatchlings to get out but not for the other animals to get in.

4. If we have to move a nest, we use this to help us dig a new nest, just like the female loggerhead.

5. The red lens helps us to use this at night without bothering the sea turtles.

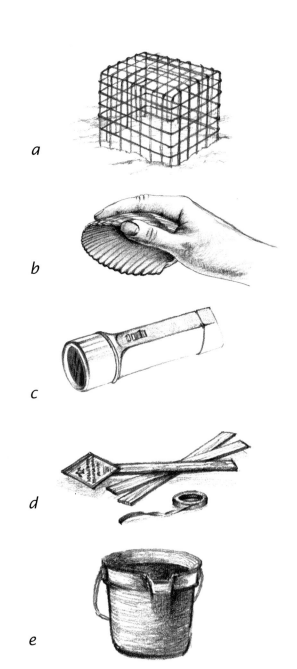

a

b

c

d

e

Can you identify the shells? Answers are upside down, below.

1 Pen Shell
2 Urchins
3 Cockle Shells
4 Clam Shell
5 Angel Wing Shell
6 Whelk Shell
7 Skate's Egg Purses
8 Molted Horseshoe Crab Shell
9 Moon Snail

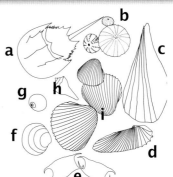

1-c, 2-b, 3-i, 4-f 5-d, 6-h, 7-e, 8-a, 9-g

Make Your Own Nature Scrapbook

Find a spot outdoors to sit and observe nature; a park, the beach, a lake, the woods – it can even be your own backyard.

Look around. Write down the words that describe what you see.

What type of day is it?

Is it windy, sunny, or cloudy? Has it just rained or snowed? Is it hot or cold?

What time of day is it? Is it early morning, noon, late afternoon or evening?

Do you know the name of that plant or bird or flower? If you don't, be careful when you describe or draw it. You can look up the name when you get home.

- What color is it?
- What size is it?
- What shapes (circles, triangles, rectangles) are there in the bird beaks, feathers, leaves, shells, rocks, or sticks, etc.?
- Is it smooth, rough, hard, soft, slimy, or scaly?
- Now close your eyes and let your other senses take over.
- What do you hear?
- What do you smell?
- What do you feel?

Now open your eyes and write everything down.

Your observation is done! Now you are ready to go back home and gather your thoughts into sentences and write or draw in your nature notebook.

If you want, add clippings, pressed flowers, leaves, etc. Photographs are fun, too!

Food for thought: Would your observations change at different times of the day or if the weather was different? If you can, try to observe the same thing at different times of the day or at the same time over several different days. Are your observations the same or different? Why or why not?